5/18

More Books That Drive Kids CRAZY!
Books That Drive Kids Crazy!: Did You Take the B from My _ook?
Books That Drive Kids Crazy!: This Is a Ball

This book is for our daughter, Bonnie.

Bonnie, you are right at the beginning of your first year of preschool and we are so proud of how brave, kind, and creative you are.
You will read so many books as you go to school. Some will be funny. Some will be sad. Some will make you want to read without stopping, because they are so wonderful.

This book, however, is just for you. Mummy and Daddy love you very much. You are spectacular.

Ⓛ Ⓑ

Little, Brown and Company
New York   Boston

The illustrations for this book were drawn and colored digitally. The text was set in Sentinel.

Text and artwork copyright © 2017 by Beck and Matt Stanton • Cover art copyright © 2017 by Beck and Matt Stanton. • Cover design by Matt Stanton and Nicole Brown. Hachette Book Group supports the right to free expression and the value of copyright. The purpose of copyright is to encourage writers and artists to produce the creative works that enrich our culture. The scanning, uploading, and distribution of this book without permission is a theft of the author's intellectual property. If you would like permission to use material from the book (other than for review purposes), please contact permissions@hbgusa.com. Thank you for your support of the author's rights. • Little, Brown and Company • Hachette Book Group • 1290 Avenue of the Americas, New York, NY 10104 • Visit us at LBYR.com Originally published in 2017 by HarperCollins*Publishers* in Australia. First U.S. Edition: April 2018 • Little, Brown and Company is a division of Hachette Book Group, Inc. The Little, Brown name and logo are trademarks of Hachette Book Group, Inc. • The publisher is not responsible for websites (or their content) that are not owned by the publisher. • Library of Congress Cataloging-in-Publication Data • Names: Stanton, Beck, author, illustrator. | Stanton, Matt, 1988– author, illustrator. Title: This book is red / by Beck Stanton and Matt Stanton. Description: First U.S. edition. | New York ; Boston : Little, Brown and Company, 2018. | Series: Books that drive kids crazy! ; 3 | Originally published in 2017 by HarperCollins*Publishers* in Australia. | Summary: "In this humorous concept book, readers are asked to question their logic for naming colors"—Provided by publisher. • Identifiers: LCCN 2017022921 | ISBN 9780316434492 (hardcover) | ISBN 9780316434485 (ebook) | ISBN 9780316434478 (library edition ebook) Subjects: | CYAC: Color—Fiction. | Red—Fiction. | Humorous stories. Classification: LCC PZ7.1.S737 Thi 2018 | DDC [E]—dc23 LC record available at https://lccn.loc.gov/2017022921 PRINTED IN CHINA APS • 10 9 8 7 6 5 4 3 2 1 ISBNs: 978-0-316-43449-2 (hardcover), 978-0-316-43448-5 (ebook), 978-0-316-47886-1 (ebook), 978-0-316-47894-6 (ebook)

Hello!

Let's read this book together.

**First, I need to check
a few things.**

**What color is
this crown?**

**What color is
this tie?**

**What color are
these glasses?**

Nope!

They are all RED!

**And by the end of this book
you will think they are red too.**

**Not only that, you will
know that this book is red.**

**Watch closely.
Are you paying attention?**

Okay. Let's do this.

This is Barney.
He is a lobster.

He is red, right?

Yes! We agree. What a great way to start.

This is Fergus.
He is a frog.

He is also red.

He's as red as red can be.

Barney and Fergus are the same color.

Obviously.

They are, and I will tell you why.

It is a well-known
fact that Barney
only <u>ever</u> wears
red clothes.

So the tie he is
wearing must
be red.

He wears ruby red and fire-truck red.
You should see his closet! It is full of
all the red clothes he can get his nippers on.

I'm sure you'd agree
that Fergus is
the same color
as Barney's tie, yes?

So Fergus is red too.

No, no. The tie has to be red, remember?
Barney wouldn't be caught dead wearing
something that wasn't red.

You need more proof?

Fergus is the same color as this apple.

Apples are red.

See!
Fergus <u>must</u> be red.

You're just not getting this, are you ...

Let me introduce you to my penguin friend.

Her name is Rose.

Say hello to Rose.

Rose says it's very nice to meet you. Now, you really need to switch on your listening ears and watching eyes. This is very simple, but you tend to miss things.

Roses are red.

So Rose the penguin is red.

Are you calling me a liar?
Ouch.

Red Rose is wearing glasses.

Her glasses are red.

They are the same color that you can see on the front of this book.

But this is called *This Book Is Red.*
It has to be red.
Have you lost your marbles?

Okay,
I know you
don't think this
book is red,
but remember
you thought
Fergus was green!

Oh, come on! He's not green!
Nothing about Fergus is green.

Sometimes we all get things wrong. We're only human, after all.

I mean, you didn't even think Barney's tie was red. But everything here is red!

Oh! Look! There they are on the floor. Your marbles. It seems you <u>have</u> lost them.

When you were a baby you thought spoons were airplanes.

You were wrong then and you're wrong now!

I hate to be the one to tell you, but you have really lost it.

All right,
that's enough.
I am the grown-up.

What I say goes.

THEY ARE RED BECAUSE I SAID SO!

Let me tell you
something we
do agree on, then.

This book is
definitely red.

For the Grown-Ups:

Okay, people.
We have a challenge for you.

It's your job to convince
the nearest kid that
everything in this book
is actually red.

And we mean everything.

It will not be easy!
Kids will try to persuade you
that things are not as red as you
say, but you will stay strong!

And the kids will love it!

Here are two more books that will
DRIVE KIDS CRAZY:

$14.99 U.S. / $19.99 CAN.

This
book is
RED

Seriously?

BOOKS THAT DRIVE KIDS CRAZY!

Beck & Matt Stanton

Stanton

Books That Drive Kids CRAZY! • This book is RED

Yes, it is.
We just read it.